An I Can Read Book®

DIGBY

story by Barbara Shook Hazen
pictures by Barbara J. Phillips-Duke

HarperCollins*Publishers*

HarperCollins®, ☛®, and I Can Read® are trademarks
of HarperCollins Publishers, Inc.

Digby
Text copyright © 1997 by Barbara Shook Hazen
Illustrations copyright © 1997 by Barbara J. Phillips-Duke
Manufactured in China. All rights reserved.
For information address HarperCollins Children's Books,
a division of HarperCollins Publishers, 195 Broadway,
New York, NY 10007.

Library of Congress Cataloging-in-Publication Data
Hazen, Barbara Shook.
  Digby / story by Barbara Shook Hazen ; pictures by Barbara J. Phillips-Duke.
     p.   cm. — (An I can read book)
  Summary: Learning about the family dog, Digby, helps a young child
understand aging.
  ISBN 0-06-026253-2. — ISBN 0-06-026254-0 (lib. bdg.)
  ISBN 0-06-444239-X (pbk.)
  [1. Dogs—Fiction. 2. Old age—Fiction.] I. Title. II. Series.
PZ7.H314975Di   1996   95-1689
[E]—dc20   CIP
                                                                  AC

15 16 17 18 SCP 20 19 18
❖
Visit us on the World Wide Web!
http://www.harperchildrens.com

To Elizabeth—delight in reading.
And to Virginia—continued delight in dogs.
—B.S.H.

To the memory of my mother, Lucy May Phillips.
To my children, Enum and Erin.
Special thank-you to Melanie, Jane, and Maggie.
Last but not least, thank you, Father.
—B.J.P.-D.

Come on, Digby.

Let's play with my new ball.

Run, Digby!

Catch the ball!

6

Digby can't play catch
with you.

Why not?

Come on, Digby.

You can do it!

Digby is too old

to play catch with you.

9

How do you know?

Because I am older
and I know more.

Digby is too old to play.

See the way she walks?

11

How old is Digby?

Old for a dog.

Digby was here

before I was born.

Here is a picture of her

with me when I was little.

Did Digby play with you?

Yes, and Digby helped me

learn to walk.

Did Digby help me walk?

16

No, I helped you walk.

What else did you and Digby do?

We played catch.

Digby ran very fast.

Sometimes she hid the ball.

Could Digby do tricks?

Could she roll over?

Yes, and Digby could shake

and jump a stick.

Jump, Digby!

I told you

Digby can't jump now.

She is too old to jump.

What can Digby do now?

She can still shake and go for walks.

And she can still be our friend.

Digby can do other things
better now.

What other things?

She is better at waiting

and watching us play.

She is better at understanding.

I still wish she could play

catch with me.

Digby can't, but I can.

I can show you how to catch.

Can you show me how to catch
like you do?

I can show you how to catch

like Digby did.

You'll have to practice a lot

to be as good as I am.

Come on, Digby!

Come watch us play!